A NOTE TO PARENTS

Disney's **First Readers Level 1** books were developed with the beginning reader in mind. They feature large, easy-to-read type, lots of repetition, and simple vocabulary.

One of the most important ways parents can help their child develop a love of reading is by providing an *environment* for reading. Every time you discuss a book, read aloud to your child, or your child observes you reading, you promote the development of early reading skills and habits. Here are some tips to help you use **Disney's First Readers Level 1** books with your child:

★ Tell the story about the original Disney film or video. Storytelling is crucial to language development. A young child needs a language *foundation* before reading skills can begin to emerge.

★ Talk about the illustrations in the book. Beginning readers need to use illustrations to gather clues about unknown words or to understand the story.

★ Read aloud to your child. When you read aloud, run your finger smoothly under the text. Do not stop at each word. Enliven the text for your child by using a different voice for each character. In other words, be an actor—and have fun!

★ "Read it again!" Children love hearing stories read again and again. When they begin reading on their own, repetition helps them feel successful. Maintain patience, be encouraging, and expect to read the same books over and over.

★ Play "question and answer." Use the After-Reading Fun activities provided at the end of each book to further enhance your child's learning process.

Remember that early-reading experiences that you share with your child can help him or her to become a confident and successful reader later on!

— Patricia Koppman
Past President
International Reading Association

First published by Random House, Inc., New York, New York.
This edition published by Scholastic Inc.,
90 Old Sherman Turnpike, Danbury, Connecticut 06816
by arrangement with Disney Licensed Publishing.

SCHOLASTIC and associated logos are trademarks
and/or registered trademarks of Scholastic Inc.

ISBN 0-7172-6053-4

Printed in the U.S.A.

FINDING NEMO

Disney · PIXAR

BEST DAD IN THE SEA

by Amy J. Tyler
Illustrated by the Disney Storybook Artists
Designed by Disney's Global Design Group

Disney's First Readers — Level 1
A Story from Disney/Pixar's *Finding Nemo*

SCHOLASTIC INC.

New York   Toronto   London   Auckland   Sydney
Mexico City   New Delhi   Hong Kong   Buenos Aires

Nemo loves his dad,
Marlin.
And Marlin loves Nemo.

But they are very different.

Marlin is careful.
"Slow down, Nemo!"
Nemo is not.
"Come on, Dad!"

One day, Nemo is
TOO brave.

He swims out
to the open sea.

Oh, no! A diver.
Marlin cannot see Nemo.

Nemo has been caught!

Marlin swims
after Nemo.
But he is too late.

PLOP!
Into a tank Nemo goes.

How will he ever
get home?

Marlin is sad.
He wants to search
for Nemo.
His new friend Dory
can help.

At first,
Marlin is very,
very afraid.

But not for long.
"My son needs me!"
Marlin says.

For Nemo,
Marlin is brave.

He is VERY brave!

Nemo hears
good news.
Help is on the way.

Nemo escapes!
Dory finds Nemo first.
They look for his dad.

They ask the crabs
for help.

They find Marlin. But
Dory gets caught in a net.
Nemo has a plan.

He swims into the net.
"Swim down!" he says to
the other fish.
They swim deep into the
ocean. The net breaks free!

"You were so brave,"
says Nemo.
"You were brave, too,"
says his dad.

Nemo loves his dad.
And his dad loves him.

And they are not
so different after all!

Enhance the reading experience with follow-up questions to help your child develop reading comprehension and increase his/her awareness of words.

Approach this with a sense of play. Make a game of having your child answer the questions. You do not need to ask all the questions at one time. Let these questions be fun discussions rather than a test. If your child doesn't have instant recall, encourage him/her to look back into the book to "research" the answers. You'll be modeling what good readers do and, at the same time, forging a sharing bond with your child.

1. How are Nemo and his dad, Marlin, different?

2. What happens to Nemo when he swims ahead of his dad?

3. Who helps Marlin search for Nemo?

4. How do Nemo and Dory escape from the net?

5. How are Nemo and Marlin similar?

6. Name one way in which you are similar to your mom or dad. Name one way in which you are different from your mom or dad.

Answers: 1. *Possible answers:* Marlin is careful; Nemo is not careful. Marlin swims slowly; Nemo swims quickly. 2. He is caught by a diver and put in a fish tank. 3. Dory. 4. Nemo tells the fish in the net to swim down so that the net breaks free from the boat. 5. *Possible answers:* They are both brave. They both love each other. 6. Answers will vary.